8-14
P9-BZL-560

FOURTH OF JULY MICE!

Fourth of July Mice!

by Bethany Roberts

Illustrated by Doug Cushman

Green Light Readers
Houghton Mifflin Harcourt
Boston New York

First Green Light Readers edition, 2014

www.hmhco.com

The Library of Congress has cataloged the hardcover edition as follows:
Roberts, Bethany.
Fourth of July Mice!/by Bethany Roberts; illustrated by Doug Cushman
p.cm.
Summary: Four energetic mice enjoy a parade and other festivities on Independence Day.
[1. Fourth of July—Fiction. 2. Mice—Fiction. 3. Stories in rhyme.]
I. Cushman, Doug, ill. II. Title.
Pz8.3.R515Fo 2004
[E]—dc22 2003013163

ISBN: 978-0-618-31366-2 hardcover
ISBN: 978-0-544-22605-0 GLR paperback
ISBN: 978-0-544-23600-4 GLR paper over board

Manufactured in China
SCP 10 9 8 7 6 5 4 3

4500480000

Happy Birthday, America!
—B.R.

To Leonard Everett Fisher
—painter, patriot, teacher, and friend
—D.C.

Parading mice
march left, right, left.

Waving flags,
red, white, and blue!

Bang! Toot! Clang!
Happy Fourth!

Mr. Mouse
marches too.

Hungry mice
left, right . . . stop!

It's time to eat.
What's for lunch?

Sunflower seeds!
Pass the cheese!

Munch, munch,
crunch, crunch, crunch!

Now let's play!
Toss the ball.

Whack, smack,
run, run, run!

Let's have a race!

Four mice in sacks

hop, hop, plop.
Oh, what fun!

Three hot mice
in red, white, blue

plunk, dunk,
one, two, three.

One scared mouse
stays on the bank,
shaking, quaking.

"No, not me!"

Three wet mice
dip, float, glide.

Drip, flop, flip,
splash, splosh, slide.

One dry mouse suns on a rock.
Mr. Mouse sails—glide, ride.

“Stop, Mr. Mouse! You’ve gone too far!”
Oh no! What to do?

A brave little mouse
jumps right in.

"I can swim!"

"Three cheers for you!"

Four happy mice
sparkle on a log.

Is mouse fun done
this July Fourth day?

Look in the sky . . .
BOOM! BOOM! BOOM!

We love America!
Hooray! Hooray!